An I Can Read Book®

GREG'S MICROSCOPE

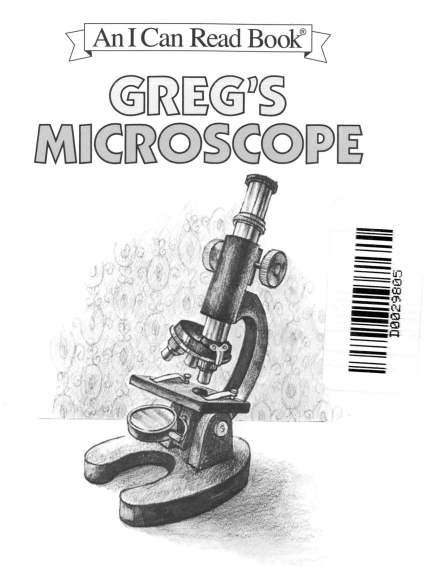

by Millicent E. Selsam
pictures by Arnold Lobel

HarperCollinsPublishers

To Gregory Hunt

HarperCollins®, 📖®, and I Can Read Book®
are trademarks of HarperCollins Publishers Inc.

Greg's Microscope
Text copyright © 1963 by Millicent E. Selsam
Text copyright renewed 1991 by Millicent E. Selsam
Pictures copyright © 1963 by Arnold Lobel
Pictures copyright renewed 1991 by Adam Lobel
For information address HarperCollins Children's Books,
a division of HarperCollins Publishers,
195 Broadway, New York, NY 10007.
Manufactured in China.
LC 63-8002
ISBN 0-06-444144-X (pbk.)
14 15 16 17 SCP 20 19 18

GREG'S MICROSCOPE

Greg wanted a microscope.

"Father," he said,

"buy me a microscope, please."

"What for?" asked his father.

"So I can see tiny things," said Greg.

"Can't you see tiny things without

a microscope?" asked his father.

"Look at this spot.

It is tiny.

Look at this ant.

It is tiny.

What do you want to see?"

"Well," said Greg,

"Billy has a microscope.

It came in a box

with some glass slides.

He can see the hairs

on a spider's foot.

He can see the little hooks

in a bird's feather.

They are tiny.

But they look big

under the microscope.

I want to see those things, too."

"Can't you look

through Billy's microscope?"

asked Greg's father.

"He is using it.

I need my own," said Greg.

"I will have to think about that,"

said his father.

"Microscopes cost a lot of money."

"Oh," said Greg.

"Billy's father did not pay a lot."

"I will speak to him,"

said Greg's father.

Greg's father spoke to Billy's father.

Then he began to shop

for a microscope.

He went to the toy stores.

He went to the big department stores.

He went to a place

where they sold used microscopes.

He came home with a big box.

"Greg," he called.

Greg came running.

"What is in that box?" he asked.

"Open it and see," said his father.

Greg opened the box.

"Wow!" he said. "What a microscope.

Did you pay a lot?" Greg asked.

"Not too much," said his father.

Greg's father put the microscope

on the table in front of the window.

"Look into it," he said.

Greg sat down.

He looked into it.

"I can't see anything.

It is all dark," he said.

"Move the mirror at the bottom

till it catches the light,"

said his father.

Greg moved the mirror.

"I can see now," he said.

"Well, Greg," said his father.

"Look at tiny things."

Greg sat still.

"Didn't you buy some slides

for me to look at?"

"No, Greg," said his father.

"Find your own tiny things."

"What shall I look at?" asked Greg.

"What is tiny?"

He ran into the kitchen.

"Mother," he said, "please give me some tiny things to look at."

His mother was holding the salt box.

"Try some salt," she said.

Greg ran back and got a glass slide.

He put some salt on it.

Then he went to the microscope.

He put the slide on.

"Wait," called Greg's father.

"I will show you how to use it."

He showed Greg

how to move the wheels

until he could see the salt.

"The salt looks like big blocks,"

Greg said.

"Well," said his father.

"The salt looks 100 times bigger
than it really is."

"100 times bigger!" said Greg.

Greg's mother came in.

"Let me see that salt," she said.

She looked through the microscope.

"My goodness," she said.

"The salt looks like rocks.

Come into the kitchen, Greg.

Let's look for more tiny things."

Greg did not go right away.

He just kept looking at the salt.

"Add some water," said his father.

Greg got some water

and put a drop on the salt.

Then he looked into the microscope.

"Father," he cried,

"the salt is getting

smaller and smaller.

It's going.

It's going.

It's gone!

My salt is gone!" said Greg.

"Where did it go?"

"It went into the water,"

said his father.

"Put the slide in the sun.

Let it dry."

Greg put the slide in the sun.

Then he took another slide

and went into the kitchen.

"Let's try some sugar,"

he said to his mother.

Greg's mother gave him some sugar.

Greg put it on the slide.

Then he went back to look at it
through the microscope.

"Sugar looks like blocks, too.

But these blocks are not as even

as the salt blocks," he said.

"Add some water," said his father.

"No," said Greg. "I lost the salt.

I will lose the sugar, too."

"See if your salt slide is dry,"

said his father.

Greg looked.

"Father," he said.

"The salt came out of the water.

It is back on the slide.

But it looks different."

"You get better crystals when

they form in water,"

said his father.

"Crystals!" said Greg.

"What are they?"

"Look at them and see,"

said his father.

Greg put the slide on the microscope.

"Oh," he said.

"The salt looks

like glass blocks now."

24

"Let me look," said his father,

"and call Mother."

Greg went to get his mother.

His mother looked

through the microscope.

"Almost like diamonds," she said.

"That's right," said Greg's father.

"Every little crystal of sugar and salt

has sharp corners,

just like diamonds."

"Do all crystals have sharp corners?"

asked Greg.

"Yes," said his father.

"Let's see some good sugar crystals,"

said Greg.

He put some water on the sugar.

He looked through the microscope.

Each little block

got smaller and smaller.

"They are going-going-gone," said Greg.

He put the slide in the sun.

He looked at it when it was dry.

The sugar looked like glass flowers.

"What beautiful crystals," Greg said.

"Now let's look at pepper."

He put some pepper on a slide

and looked at it.

"No crystals here," he said.

"Pepper looks like dirt."

The next day was a holiday.

Greg's friend Billy came to the door.

"Come and see my new microscope,"

said Greg.

"This is a good one," Billy said.

"Let me see some slides."

"I made my own," said Greg.

And he showed Billy

the salt and sugar slides.

Billy looked.

"Those are crystals," said Greg.

"Every little crystal of sugar and salt

has sharp corners, like diamonds."

"Is everything made of crystals?"

asked Billy.

"No," said Greg. "Look at pepper."

Billy looked at the pepper.

"Let's look at more things," he said.

"How about flour?

Did you look at flour?

How about butter? And milk?"

"One thing at a time," said Greg.

He got a little flour

and put it on a slide.

"Add a drop of water," said Billy.

"Will the flour go into the water?"

asked Greg.

"I don't know," said Billy.

Greg put water on the flour.

He looked through the microscope.

"No," he said.

"The flour stays there."

"Don't you have a cover glass?" asked Billy.

"Put a cover glass on."

"Why?" asked Greg.

"You will see better," said Billy.

Greg started to put

the cover glass on.

Billy watched.

"Don't plop it on," he said.

"Why not?" asked Greg.

"You will get too many air bubbles,"

said Billy.

"Good! I want to see

what they look like," said Greg.

"Oh, you will see," said Billy.

"Just plop the cover glass on."

Greg did just that.

Then he looked at the slide.

"What are those big black circles?"

asked Greg.

"Air bubbles," said Billy.

"I like them!" said Greg.

"Where is the flour?"

"Let me see," said Billy.

"Those little clear things

must be the flour."

Just then Greg's mother came in.

"Flour?" she said.

"Let me see what it looks like.

I see black rings."

"Those are air bubbles," said Greg.

"Look between them.

You will see little clear things.

That is the flour."

"Greg," said his mother,

"you know so much."

"Oh, not so much," said Greg.

And he looked at Billy.

Greg's mother sat down to sew.

Greg and Billy kept looking

at different things.

They looked at butter.

They looked at milk.

They looked at dust.

Every minute Greg's mother

heard the boys say,

"Oh, look at this."

"Wow, see this."

Then they were standing near her.

"May we look at your thread?"

they asked.

"Sure," she said.

"Here is a piece of cotton thread."

Greg took the thread.

He made a slide

and looked at it.

"This is the best yet," he said.

"Look at this, Billy.

Look, Mother."

Greg's mother looked.

Billy looked.

The cotton thread was really

many threads twisted together.

"This is wonderful,"

said Greg's mother.

"Try some of my wool."

Greg put a piece of wool

under the microscope.

Each wool thread was really

many threads twisted together.

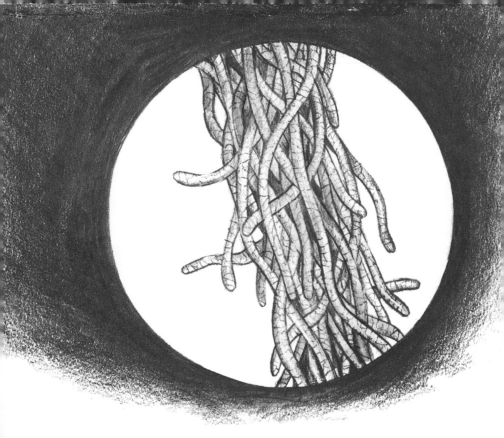

"But look, Billy," said Greg.

"Look at one of the wool threads.

It has scales all over it,

like fish scales."

Billy looked.

"Hmm," he said.

"Maybe all hair looks like that."

"Hair," cried Greg.

"What has hair to do with wool?"

"Think," said Billy.

"Where does wool come from?"

Greg thought.

"From sheep," he yelled.

"I get it. Wool is sheep hair."

"So there," said Billy.

On Monday Greg

came home from school.

He had an idea.

"I am going to look at other hairs,"

he said to his mother.

He pulled a hair from his head.

"Now I will see what it looks like,"

he said.

He made a slide.

He looked at his hair.

"Does it look like wool?"

asked his mother.

Greg looked at his mother.

"I am not a sheep," he said,

"but my hair does have scales."

"Greg," said his mother.

"I wonder what

a dog's hair looks like."

"Mother," said Greg.

"You wonder almost as much as I do.

Where will I find a dog?"

Just then the doorbell rang.

Greg went to the door.

"May I come in?" asked Mrs. Broom.

Greg looked at her dog.

"Sure, Mrs. Broom, come in. Please,"
said Greg.

"Oh, hello, Mrs. Broom,"
said Greg's mother.

"Greg! A dog! Just in time.
May we have one of Coco's hairs,
Mrs. Broom?
Greg wants to look at it
through the microscope."

"Well, in that case," said Mrs. Broom.

She looked at the sleeve of her coat.

"Here are a few," she said.

Greg took the hairs.

He put them on a slide with water
and a cover slip.

Greg looked at the slide.

"Let me see," said his mother.

"I want to see my dog's hair,"
said Mrs. Broom.

"One at a time," said Greg.

"One at a time."

Mrs. Broom looked.

His mother looked.

"It's hard to believe,"

said Mrs. Broom.

"One little hair

looks like a long pole."

Greg looked at Coco.

"Don't you want to look too?"

he asked.

But Coco just wagged his tail.

One day Greg said to his mother,

"My teacher wants me to bring

my microscope to school."

"Don't they have one?"

asked his mother.

"Not in our class," said Greg.

"Well, carry it very carefully,"

said his mother.

Greg took the microscope to school.

When he came home, he said,

"Mother, the teacher showed us

how every living thing

is made of cells."

"Cells?" said Greg's mother.

"Yes," said Greg.

"Cells are what

every living thing is made of."

"Well, show me," said Greg's mother.

"Let's get an onion," said Greg.

He peeled off the thin clear skin

from a piece of onion.

He made a slide and looked at it.

"See," he said.

"There are the cells."

Greg's mother looked.

"They are like bricks in a wall,"

she said.

"I'll show you my cells," said Greg.

"Don't cut yourself,"

said his mother.

"I won't. Just watch this."

Greg took a toothpick.

He rubbed the end of it

on the inside of his mouth.

Then he rubbed that end in a drop

of water on a slide.

He put a cover slip on it.

Then he looked through the microscope.

"Here, Mother," he said.

"These are my very own cells."

His mother looked.

"What nice cells," she said.

Greg had a new idea.

"I'm going to look at the leaves
in my fish tank," he said.

"Maybe I will see cells there, too."

Greg took a leaf from his fish tank
and made a slide.

"Green bricks,"

he called to his mother.

Then he moved the slide

to see the edge of the leaf.

"Things are moving here," he cried.

Just then Greg's father came home.

"What's for dinner?" he asked.

"I'm hungry."

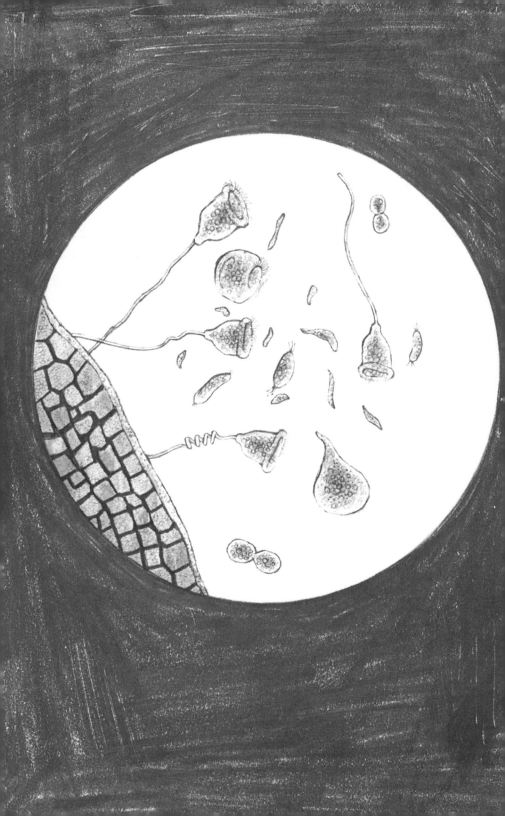

Greg's mother went to the kitchen.

"Dinner will be ready soon," she said.

"See what Greg has

under the microscope."

"Take a look," said Greg.

"It is the busiest place

you ever saw."

Greg's father looked.

"Those are animals, Greg," he said,

"and each animal

is just one single cell."

"I just learned about cells,"

said Greg.

"But I didn't know there could be

a whole animal of just one cell!

There must be a hundred of them

on that one leaf."

His father kept looking.

He looked and looked.

Greg waited.

His mother came into the room.

"Did you see this?"

asked Greg's father.

"No, let me see."

She sat down to look.

Greg waited.

Then he looked at his father.

"I told you I needed a microscope,
Father," he said.

"But I was wrong.
I think we need
three microscopes for this family."